Tell Me About It

 HOUGHTON MIFFLIN   BOSTON

Photo credits

Cover © Peter Dazeley/Getty Images. (bkgd) ©1995 PhotoDisc, Inc. All rights reserved. Images ©1995 PhotoLink. **Title** © David Young-Wolff/PhotoEdit Inc. **17** © Randy Faris/Corbis. **18** © Visions of America, LLC / Alamy. **19** © David Sacks/Getty Images. **20** © Eric Nathan/Alamy. **21** © Sami Sarkis France/Alamy. **22** © Radius Images/Alamy. **23** © Phil Degginger/Alamy. **24** © Nikreates/Alamy. **65** © Phil Degginger/Alamy. **66** Tony Freeman/PhotoEdit Inc. **67** © Somos Images LLC/Alamy. **68** © Image Source/Getty Images. **69** © Comstock/Corbis. **70** © David Young-Wolff/PhotoEdit Inc. **71** © 2005 Comstock/Jupiterimages. **72** © Paul Ridsdale/Alamy.

Printed in the United States of America

ISBN-13: 978-0-547-07449-8
ISBN-10: 0-547-07449-2

7 8 9 0868 15 14 13 12
4500352052

Contents

Jess Makes Gifts

by Louise Tidd
illustrated by Anne Sibley O'Brien

Jess likes to use things she has at home to make some gifts. Jess makes gifts for Mom, Dad, Mike, and Gram. Jess uses different things to make those gifts. Jess wishes that Mom, Dad, Mike, and Gram will like the gifts she makes.

1

Jess uses paper strips and makes red
roses for Mom. Jess adds stems and
places bunches of roses in vases. She puts
these roses on the table. Jess makes roses
because Mom likes roses.

In spring, Mom will plant rose plants.
Mom will make sure that the rose plants
get water and sun. Mom will be glad
when those roses grow. For now, Mom
has these paper roses.

Jess sketches and uses brushes. She makes a big sun, grass, a tan flag, and golf clubs. Jess makes them because Dad likes to play golf.

When the grass is wet, Dad cannot
play golf. Dad wishes he could, but he
cannot. Now Dad has these nice golf
pictures that Jess made and he will smile.

Jess makes boxes of different sizes for
Mike. Jess makes five boxes red and five
boxes tan. Mike will use them as blocks.
Jess makes blocks because Mike likes to
play with them.

Jess stacks the boxes. Mike makes
them crash down, and that makes him
smile. Then Mike stacks the boxes and
makes them fall. Another smile flashes
across his face.

Jess bakes muffins for Gram because she likes muffins. Jess adds things and Mom mixes them. Jess places those muffins on dishes.

Just then, Jane heard Gram come in. Gram sat and had muffins with them. Gram thanked Jane. Jane smiled. She was thinking about what to make next.

Cooking with Mom Fox

by Cesar Perez

illustrated by Barry Gott

Mom Fox makes good food. Mom Fox will give classes. Mom Fox wishes little foxes will take her classes. She hopes those classes will be fun.

Chip, Chuck, Chet, and Chad sit in
class. Mom Fox passes around boxes of
mix and some cups.

"Fill a cup with mix and place the mix
in those big dishes," Mom Fox tells them.
"Do not spill."

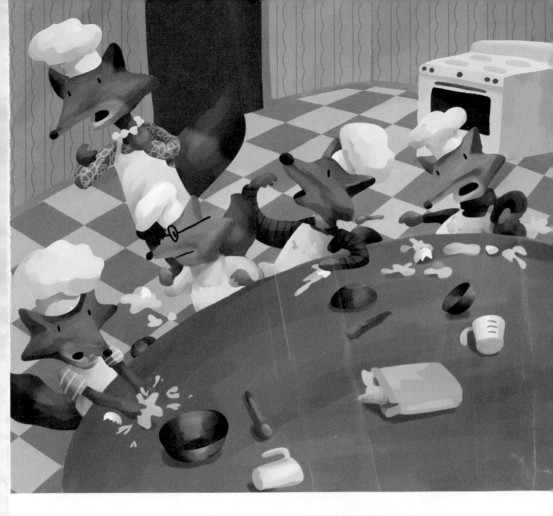

Next, Mom Fox will show how to crack eggs. Chip cracks an egg, but it smashes in his hand. Chuck cracks an egg, but drops it. Chad cracks an egg, and it drips on him. Chet cracks an egg, and it splashes all over. What a mess!

Mom Fox cracks eggs for the foxes.
"What are we making?" Chip asks.
"Will it be an egg sandwich? Will it be
an egg dumpling or an egg muffin?"
Chet asks.

"You will see," Mom Fox tells them.
The foxes add milk. They whip the
milk, eggs, and mix until it fluffs up.
  "Add five pinches of spice," Mom Fox
tells them. "Mix it well, too," she adds.

Mom Fox drops bits of the fluffed up
mix on a pan. When Mom Fox finishes,
she lets the foxes see.

"We made pancakes!" Chuck yells.

Mom Fox places pancakes on their
plates. She dashes to get napkins. The
foxes take grapes and use them to make
cute fox faces on the pancakes.

"We are great at this!" Chet yells as he munches on his pancake.

"We had a great teacher," Chuck adds.

"We'll take another class," says Chet.

"Yes, we will," says Chad.

When Mom Fox heard that, she smiled.

Trains

by Prima Secunda

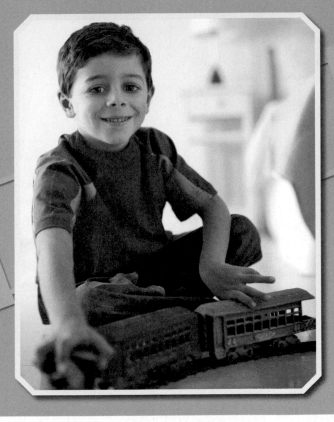

Would you say that playing with
trains is fun? Many children think that
playing with trains is fun. Children
spend time making trains zip and stop on
long, thin tracks.

Look at this gray train with its red,
white, and blue stripes. Would you like a
ride on this train?

Someone is waving. He will wait until
everyone gets on. Then he will wave to
say it is safe for the train to go.

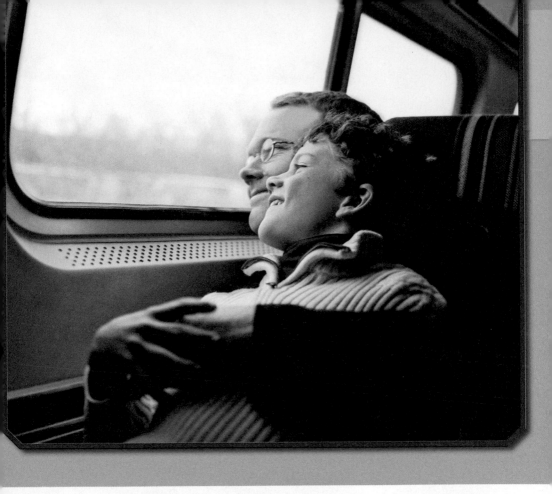

People may take train rides to visit
places. This train rides on tracks that
stay close to the water.

This boy and his dad see white waves
crashing against the sand. It is fun to be
on this train as it rides on its way.

Subway trains ride on tracks under a big city. Subway trains make stops, and people get on and off. People say that subway trains are a fast way to get places in a big city.

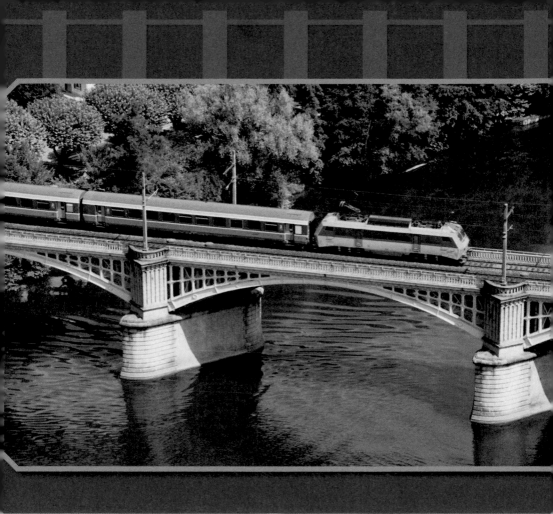

Trains can ride on tracks that go on
flat land. Trains can ride on tracks that
go on high land. This train can ride on
tracks along this bridge. What a nice ride
people can have on this train!

Trains carry people and other things.
This train will take these logs a long way.
Trains bring us mail and food. Trains
bring many things that we use every day.

A train may pass this place. This red light flashes when a train is on its way. When this red light flashes, everyone must stop and wait as the train passes.

This train is at its last stop. Everyone must get off.

This train will wait and wait until other people can get on it. Then this train will be on its way again.

The Waiting Game

by Tyler Martin
illustrated by John Nez

Gail and Gram like playing the
waiting game. Gram and Gail fix lunch
and then wait for the mail. Gram and
Gail say it is their best time of day!

Gram and Gail sat in a waiting spot
to play the waiting game. Gram and
Gail kept track of time with the big
clock. Gram and Gail liked to see if the
mail truck came on time. The big clock
chimed. DING!

At one o'clock, the mail truck drove
next to the mailbox. Down went the flap.
In went the mail, lots and lots of mail.
The mail truck drove away. "It's as plain
as day, you got mail today, Gram. We
win the waiting game," exclaimed Gail.

Gail ran and got the mail and gave it to Gram.

"No notes! Just junk mail and ads," said Gram.

"That is fine with me!" said Gail. Gail had such fun waiting with Gram and running to get mail in the mailbox!

Just then, Gram and Gail spotted a big
mail truck.

"Two in one day?" asked Gail.

"That is odd," said Gram.

This time the mail was a note for
them. It had lots and lots of stamps.
Gram handed Gail the note.

"What does it say?" asked Gram.

"Ray is on his way. Wait at the train at six o'clock," said Gail. Gail jumped up and gave Gram a hug and kiss. That note made Gail and Gram glad!

Gail and Gram went to wait for Ray
and the train. Gail played the waiting
game with Gram. Three trains passed
them on the rails and didn't stop. Gram
and Gail waited and waited and waited.

At last, the waiting game ended at six o'clock when a big train with red stripes stopped. Someone jumped off and ran to Gram and Gail.

Ray gave Gram, his mom, a big hug. Dad gave Gail a big hug, too!

The Shell Sheep

by Anne Miranda
illustrated by Deborah Colvin Borgo

This is a story about a sheep named
Bev. Each day Bev went to the beach and
picked up seashells. Bev collected them.

Bev liked seashells. Bev liked to
feel them. Seashells came in such neat
shapes. Bev liked to see them. Bev liked
striped shells best. Bev liked to hear the
sea when she held big shells to her ear.

Each day, when Bev got back home,
she packed seashells in boxes and stashed
them in neat lines. Bev had boxes and
boxes and boxes of seashells stacked in
her little shed.

Last week, Bev needed a rake. When
Bev reached in the shed, boxes and boxes
of shells spilled out. It seemed like a sea
of seashells! Bev had a huge problem.
Bev had way too many seashells.

Bev liked seashells, but Bev could not keep them. The shed got full and shells fell out. That made Bev sad.

Just then, Bev spotted a shop for sale on the beach. That made Bev glad.

Bev had a plan. Bev named her
shop Shell World. Bev made lamps with
seashells. Bev made seashell frames. Bev
made seashell magnets and pencils.

Bev put an ad in the paper. It said:
"Sheep sells seashells at the seashore.
Sheep sells seashells cheap. This week,
free seashells with each visit!"

Lots and lots of sheep came to see Bev. Those sheep liked seashells as much as Bev did. Bev gave sheep free seashells each time one came in the shop. It made the sheep happy. That made Bev glad.

Reef Sees the Wide World

by Saturnino Romay
illustrated by Fian Arroyo

This story is about a seal named Reef. Like all seals, Reef spent his life swimming in the vast green sea. Reef could swim fast and dive deep.

41

Reef dreamed of seeing far off lands. Reef dreamed of seeing the big wide world, but Reef did not know which way to go to see the wide world!

Reef just stayed close to home.

One day, Reef spotted a bird bobbing on the waves. It flapped and flapped its wings, but it could not lift off. Reef dove in and swam at top speed to it.

"May I help?" asked Reef.

Reef helped that bird get back to his stretch of beach.

"Stay with me. Take it easy. Rest until you feel well," said Reef.

"Thanks. I'm Squeak," said Squeak.

"I'm Reef," said Reef.

Squeak needed to eat and sleep. Reef fixed Squeak a big meal. Squeak ate well and then lay in a nice safe spot to sleep. Reef felt glad he had helped Squeak.

Reef spent the next day chatting with Squeak. Squeak had seen the big wide world. She had lots of tales to tell.

Her tales made Reef think of his dream. He asked Squeak to help him get to far off lands.

Reef and Squeak planned a long trip to lands with green trees, green grass, and beaches with white sand.

In time, Squeak felt well and her wings felt strong. It was time for Reef to swim away with Squeak.

Reef dove in the deep green sea. He swam as Squeak led the way. Reef and Squeak went to those far lands. At long last, Reef got his wish to see the wide world, and he saw it with his pal!

Bill E. Goat and Wise Crow

by Chenile Evans

illustrated by Lorinda Bryan Cauley

The wind felt so cold. White snow hid
the green grass. Bill E. Goat did not like
this cold and snow. He liked to be warm.
"Hot oats will be so good," Bill E. said.

Bill E. Goat ran to the shed where he kept his oats. Bill E. could not fill his bowl with oats. He must go and get more oats at The Old Oat Shop.

He wished he did not need to go out on such a cold day.

Bill E. Goat tucked his long hair inside
his yellow hat. He put on his green coat
and his red mittens. He set off in snow so
deep that he could not see the road. Bill
E. Goat went left, but he needed to go the
other way.

Bill E. Goat had made a mistake by not going left. He went on and on in the deep snow. He ended up in a thick grove of trees. He did not know which way to go. He began to get cold. Bill E. Goat wished he had stayed home.

Just then, Bill E. Goat spotted his old pal Wise Crow. "Can you please help me get to The Old Oat Shop?" Bill E. asked.

"Yes, if you will bake me a big oat cake," said Wise Crow. She winked.

Bill E. Goat smiled and nodded "Yes."

Wise Crow flapped her wings and
began to fly fast.

"I can't keep up with that speed. This
snow makes me slow," yelled Bill E. Goat.

Wise Crow came back. "We are close.
Follow me," she said.

Bill E. Goat felt so glad to be inside
The Old Oat Shop. It was nice and warm.
Nan Goat sold him three sacks of oats.
Bill E. Goat paid for them at the front of
The Old Oat Shop. Then Bill E. Goat and
Wise Crow went to bake oat cakes.

Bill E. Goat made Wise Crow a big
stack of hot oat cakes. He and Wise Crow
both ate loads of oat cakes.

Bill E. Goat told Wise Crow "Thank
you" over and over.

Mud Bugs

by Tyler Martin

illustrated by Dominic Catalano

Eb and Flo were both yellow bugs with black stripes, but you would not know it. Eb and Flo had just played in the mud. Eb and Flo had the most mud on them that two bugs could get!

Eb had clumps of mud on his feet and hands. Eb had no yellow stripes showing. Flo also had globs of mud on her back and legs. Flo had one yellow stripe showing. Both bugs needed a bath!

The bugs spotted a nice place that had
a big green bathtub with no one in it.
The bath seemed so warm and inviting!
It had lots of foam that smelled just like
roses. Will the bugs get in?

"We must test to see if bugs with mud on them will float," said Flo.

"No way! I'm going in! Bugs always float," said Eb. He dove in, but he did not float back up like he always did. Eb had to kick his feet to stay up.

Flo followed Eb in. She didn't float like she always did. She had to kick and kick to stay up as well.

"I told you so! Bugs with mud can't float. We will sink if we don't get help," said Flo.

"Hello, hello! We need help, Flo can't float!" yelled Eb.

"We both can't float!" yelled Flo.

"Hold on! Help is on its way," said a pig with long gold hair. She was holding some soap in her hand.

"I'm going to throw the soap in the
tub. It will float. Grab the soap and get
on it!" she said.

The soap splashed and landed in front
of Eb. It floated just like a boat. Eb got
on it and lifted Flo up on the soap boat.

Both bugs thanked the pig time and
time again. At last, it was time to go.
Eb and Flo went back home safe and
clean, thanks to the pig who had that
soap that floats!

What Does It Say?

by Suzanne Martinucci

That made you stop, didn't it? When you see this at street crossings, stop! Don't cross that street until you know it is safe. A grownup has that job and will tell you when it is safe.

Roz had a thought to tell Gram. Sam
and Roz wrote Gram a note. Sam helped
Roz send this note by dropping it in a
mailbox. When Gram reads it, she will
be glad that Sam and Roz care about her.
Then Gram will write back to them.

Val can send mail without a mailbox!
Val sends mail on dad's laptop. Mom and
Dad helped Val write to Granddad on the
laptop. Then, Val pushed "Send." Her
mail, with a family snapshot, was on its
way in no time!

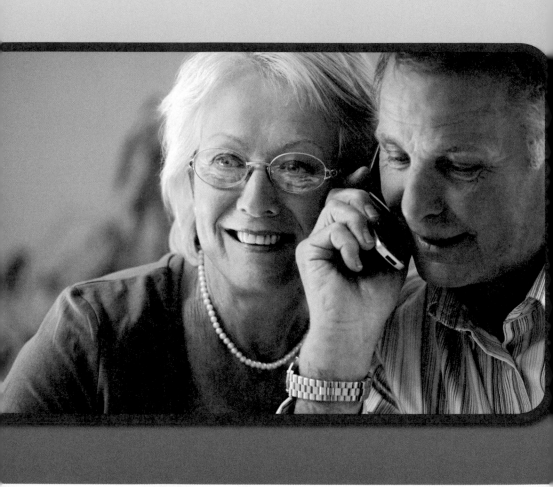

Gram and Gramps like speaking each week on the phone with their grandchild Blake. Blake began Grade 2 this week. He is telling Gram and Gramps about his classroom and his classmates.

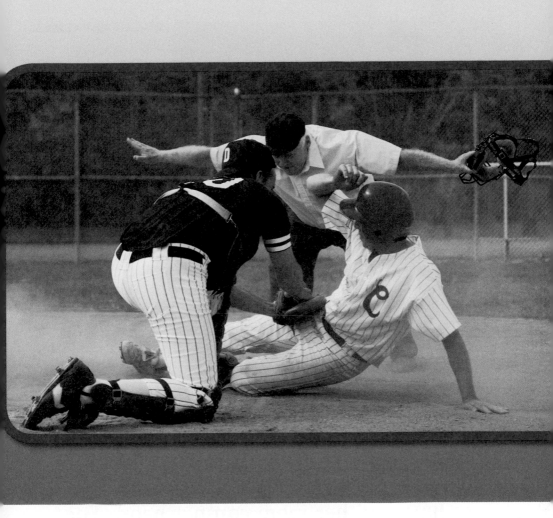

This man speaks like you speak, but
he uses his hands, too. On this play,
someone slides into home base. This man
uses his hands to show that the man who
slid is safe.

June and her mom can not hear. Each
uses her hands to speak. Mom sees what
June says with her hands. Each way
June holds those hands means something.
Mom asks June if she had fun at camp.
June tells Mom a joke.

Can you read these bumps? Maybe
not, but someone who can not see can
read these bumps by feeling them. These
bumps are a way of writing. People who
can not see can read this writing. Each
set of bumps has a meaning.

Many things in this world tell us things, but do not speak. Sunrises and sunsets tell us when a day begins and ends. Rainbows do not ever speak, but rainbows tell us that the rain has stopped.

In the Grove

by Anne Miranda
illustrated by Diane Magnuson

Gramp had a nice grove of chestnut trees on his land. It was time, at last, to collect chestnuts. So, Gramp invited his grandchildren to collect and roast the ripe chestnuts on his land.

His grandsons, Edwin and James, came
to help. Edwin liked plants, but James
liked animals best. James liked hunting
insects, not picking chestnuts. Edwin
could not wait to begin! James thought
he should have stayed at home.

"When chestnuts get ripe, the pods drop. The big problem is that chestnut pods have spines. Never pick chestnuts up with your hands. Use tongs," instructed Gramp as he handed them each a big pail and tongs.

"Take care! Old Toad has his home
close by," said Gramp.

"Old Toad?" asked James.

"Maybe you can spot him beneath a
pod. He is this big!" said Gramp.

James began picking up pods and
placing them in his pail. He hunted for
Old Toad. When James had filled his
pail, he spotted a big black hole. He
peeked in. Old Toad peeked back.

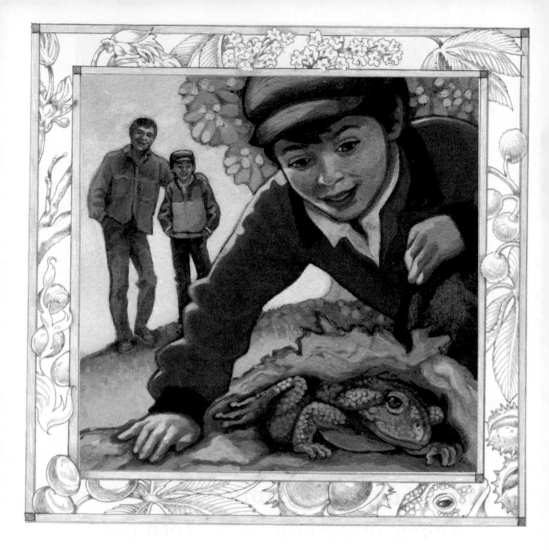

The smell of roasting chestnuts filled
the grove. Gramp, Edwin, and James ate
hot chestnuts. Then James saw Old Toad
dig back in his toad hole. James had a
fun day after all.

Word Lists

WEEK 1

Jess Makes Gifts

page 1

Decodable Words
Target Skill: *Base words with endings
-s, -es*
bakes, blocks, boxes, brushes, bunches,
clubs, dishes, gifts, muffins, places,
plants, roses, sizes, sketches, stacks,
strips, things, vases, wishes

Words Using Previously Taught Skills
adds, and, as, at, be, bug, but, cannot,
crash, Dad, different, face, five, flag,
flashes, get, glad, golf, Gram, grass,
had, has, he, him, his, home, in, is,
Jess, just, like, likes, made, make,
makes, Mike, mixes, Mom, next, nice,
on, paper, plant, red, rose, sat, she,
smile, smiled, spring, stems, sun, table,
tan, thanked, that, them, then, these,
thinking, those, use, uses, wet, when,
will, with

High-Frequency Words
New
another, heard, some

Previously Taught
a, about, across, because,
come, could, down, fall,
for, grow, now, of, pictures,
play, puts, sure, the, to, was,
water, what

WEEK 1

Cooking with Mom Fox

page 9

Decodable Words
Target Skill: *Base words with endings -s, -es*
boxes, chefs, classes, cups, dashes, dishes, eggs, faces, foxes, grapes, napkins, pancakes, pinches, plates, spice

Words Using Previously Taught Skills
add, adds, an, and, as, asks, at, be, big, bits, but, Chad, Chet, Chip, Chuck, class, crack, cracks, cup, cute, drips, drops, dumpling, egg, fill, finishes, five, fluffed, fluffs, Fox, fun, get, had, hand, he, him, his, hopes, in, is, it, lets, made, make, making, mess, milk, mix, Mom, muffin, munches, must, next, not, on, pan, pancake, passes, place, places, salt, sandwich, she, sit, smashes, smiled, spill, splashes, take, tells, that, them, those, toss, until, up, use, we, well, we'll, when, whip, will, wishes, with, yells, yes

High-Frequency Words
New
another, heard, some

Previously Taught
a, all, are, around, for, give, great, her, how, little, of, or, over, says, see, show, teacher, the, their, they, to, too, what, you

Trains

Decodable Words
Target Skill: *Vowel digraphs ai, ay*
day, gray, mail, may, playing, say, stay, subway, train, trains, wait, way

Words Using Previously Taught Skills
and, as, at, be, big, bridge, bring, can, child, close, crashing, dad, every, fast, flashes, flat, fun, get, gets, go, he, his, in, is, it, its, land, last, like, logs, long, make, making, must, nice, on, pass, passes, place, places, red, ride, rides, safe, sand, spend, stop, stops, stripes, take, that, then, these, thin, things, think, this, time, tracks, under, until, us, use, visit, wave, waves, waving, we, when, white, will, with, zip

High-Frequency Words
New
against, along, someone

Previously Taught
a, again, are, blue, boy, carry, children, city, everyone, food, for, go, have, high, light, look, many, off, other, people, see, the, to, water, what, would, you

The Waiting Game

page 25

Decodable Words
Target Skill: *Vowel digraphs ai, ay*
day, exclaimed, Gail, mail, mailbox,
plain, play, played, playing, rails, Ray,
train, trains, wait, waited, waiting, way

Words Using Previously Taught Skills
ads, and, as, asked, at, best, big, came,
chimed, clock, Dad, didn't, ding, drove,
ended, fine, fix, flap, fun, game, gave,
get, glad, got, Gram, had, handed, his,
hug, if, in, is, it, it's, jumped, junk, just,
kept, kiss, last, like, liked, lots, lunch,
made, me, mom, next, note, notes,
o'clock, odd, off, on, passed, ran, red,
running, sat, say, six, spot, spotted,
stamps, stop, stopped, stripes, such,
that, them, then, this, three, time, track,
truck, up, we, went, when, win, with

High-Frequency Words
New
someone

Previously Taught
a, away, does, down, for,
no, of, one, said, see, the,
their, to, today, too, two,
was, what, you

84

The Shell Sheep

Decodable Words

Target Skill: *Vowel digraphs ee, ea*
beach, cheap, each, ear, feel, free,
hear, keep, neat, needed, reached,
sea, seashell, seashells, seashore, see,
seemed, sheep, week

Words Using Previously Taught Skills

ad, an, and, as, at, back, best, Bev, big,
boxes, but, came, day, did, fell, frames,
gave, glad, got, had, held, her, home,
huge, in, is, it, just, lamps, last, like,
liked, lines, lots, made, magnets, much,
named, not, on, packed, pencils, picked,
plan, problem, rake, sad, sale, sells,
shapes, she, shed, shell, shells, shop,
spilled, spotted, stacked, stashed,
striped, such, that, them, then, this,
those, time, up, visit, way, went, when,
with

High-Frequency Words

New
about, story, world

Previously Taught
a, could, for, full, happy,
little, many, of, one, out,
paper, put, said, the, to, too

Reef Sees the Wide World
page 41

Decodable Words
Target Skill: *Vowel digraphs ee, ea*
beach, beaches, deep, dream, dreamed, easy, eat, feel, green, meal, needed, Reef, sea, seal, seals, see, seeing, seen, sleep, speed, Squeak, trees

Words Using Previously Taught Skills
and, as, asked, at, ate, back, big, bobbing, but, chatting, close, day, did, dive, dove, fast, felt, fixed, flapped, get, glad, got, grass, had, has, help, helped, him, his, home, in, is, it, its, just, lands, last, lay, led, life, lift, like, long, lots, made, may, named, next, nice, not, off, on, pal, planned, rest, safe, sand, she, spent, spot, spotted, stay, stayed, stretch, strong, swam, swim, swimming, take, tales, tell, thanks, that, then, think, this, those, time, top, trip, until, vast, waves, way, well, went, which, white, wide, wings, wish, with

High-Frequency Words
New
about, story, world

Previously Taught
a, all, away, bird, could, far, for, go, he, her, I, I'm, know, me, of, one, said, saw, the, to, was, you

Bill E. Goat and Wise Crow
page 49

Decodable Words
Target Skill: *Long o, oa, ow*
both, bowl, close, coat, cold, Crow, follow, go, Goat, going, grove, home, loads, oat, oats, old, over, road, slow, snow, so, sold, told, yellow

Words Using Previously Taught Skills
and, asked, at, ate, back, bake, be, being, big, Bill, but, cake, cakes, came, can, can't, day, deep, did, ended, fast, felt, fill, flapped, get, glad, grass, green, had, hat, help, hid, him, his, hot, if, in, inside, it, just, keep, kept, left, like, liked, long, made, makes, mistake, mittens, must, Nan, need, needed, nice, nodded, not, on, paid, pal, please, ran, red, sacks, see, set, she, shed, Shop, smiled, speed, spotted, stack, stayed, such, thank, that, them, then, thick, this, three, trees, tucked, up, way, we, went, which, white, will, wind, wings, winked, Wise, wished, with, yelled, yes

High-Frequency Words
New
front, hair, warm

Previously Taught
a, are, began, by, could, fly, for, good, he, her, I, know, me, more, of, off, other, out, put, said, the, to, was, where, you

Mud Bugs

page 57

Decodable Words
Target Skill: *Long o, oa, ow*
boat, both, don't, dove, Flo, float, floated, floats, foam, followed, go, going, gold, hello, hold, holding, home, know, most, no, roses, showing, so, soap, throw, told, yellow

Words Using Previously Taught Skills
and, as, at, back, bath, bathtub, big, black, bugs, but, can't, clean, clumps, did, didn't, Eb, feet, get, globs, got, grab, green, had, hand, hands, help, his, I'm, if, in, inviting, is, it, its, just, kick, landed, last, legs, lifted, like, long, lots, mud, must, need, needed, nice, not, on, pig, place, played, safe, see, seemed, she, sink, smelled, splashed, spotted, stay, stripes, test, thanked, thanks, that, them, time, tub, up, way, we, well, went, will, with, yelled

High-Frequency Words
New
front, hair, warm

Previously Taught
a, again, also, always, could, he, her, I, of, one, said, some, the, to, two, was, were, who, would, you